THE FABER BOOK OF MONOLOGUES FOR WOMEN

Jane Edwardes is the Theatre Editor for *Time Out* magazine.

*by the same author*

The Faber Book of Monologues for Men

# THE FABER BOOK OF
# Monologues for Women

INTRODUCED WITH NOTES AND COMMENTARIES
BY JANE EDWARDES

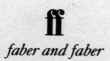

*faber and faber*

First published in 2005
by Faber and Faber Limited
3 Queen Square London WCIN 3AU
Published in the United States by Faber and Faber Inc.
an affiliate of Farrar, Straus and Giroux LLC, New York

Typeset by Country Setting, Kingsdown, Kent CT14 8ES
Printed in England by Mackays of Chatham plc, Chatham, Kent

A CIP record for this book is available from the British Library

ISBN 0-571-21765-6

2 4 6 8 10 9 7 5 3 1

# Contents

Introduction  vii

Baglady  FRANK MCGUINNESS  3
Been So Long  CHÉ WALKER  7
The Breath of Life  DAVID HARE  11
The Country  MARTIN CRIMP  17
Decadence  STEVEN BERKOFF  21
The Fastest Clock in the Universe  PHILIP RIDLEY  27
Frozen  BRYONY LAVERY  31
In Flame  CHARLOTTE JONES  35
The Late Middle Classes  SIMON GRAY  39
Medea Redux (from *Bash*)  NEIL LABUTE  43
The Mercy Seat  NEIL LABUTE  47
Night and Day  TOM STOPPARD  51
Old Times  HAROLD PINTER  55
Our Country's Good  TIMBERLAKE WERTENBAKER  59
Outlying Islands  DAVID GREIG  63
The People are Friendly  MICHAEL WYNNE  67
Portia Coughlan  MARINA CARR  71
The Positive Hour  APRIL DE ANGELIS  75
Proof  DAVID AUBURN  79
RolePlay (from the *Damsels in Distress* trilogy)
    ALAN AYCKBOURN  83
The Secret Rapture  DAVID HARE  87
Skylight  DAVID HARE  91
Three Birds Alighting on a Field
    TIMBERLAKE WERTENBAKER  95
Wit  MARGARET EDSON  99
Yard Gal  REBECCA PRICHARD  103

Acknowledgements  107

I would like to thank all the actors and directors who talked to me about their experiences of auditioning, especially Declan Donnellan, Nicolas Kent, Max Stafford-Clark and Deborah Warner; Pamela Edwardes, Nicolas Kent again, and Andrew Powell for reading the manuscript; Peggy Paterson at Faber for all her support and encouragement; and, lastly, the dramatists whose plays I have had the pleasure of seeing and reading over many years. All mistakes are, of course, my own.

# Introduction

These twenty-five modern monologues are designed for female performers of all ages with a variety of accents. The extracts have been chosen because they have an emotional drive and energy, are revealing of character and, in many cases, tell a compelling story. Long, informative pieces have been avoided. Nobody in their right mind would choose the Archbishop of Canterbury's speech disentangling the legal justification for going to war in Shakespeare's *Henry V*; even the most extraordinary of actors struggle to make it interesting. The oldest play is Harold Pinter's *Old Times*, first seen in 1971 and frequently revived. Some extracts are drawn from established playwrights, others from the less well known and up-and-coming. All the plays have been produced in Britain – several of them all over the world – mostly beginning their careers at theatres like the Royal Court and the Bush in London, or the Traverse in Edinburgh, theatres that concentrate on new writing.

Out of interest, the names of the performers who first spoke the words onstage have been included in the introductions, although that doesn't mean that you have to look like them, or that there are not different ways of playing the part. The short introductions also provide a bit of background to the play, the crucial aspects of the plot, and something about the point at which the extract occurs. and to whom the character is talking. Where there are interjections, these have been removed to help the flow of the speech. Of course, it can't be stressed strongly enough that once you have looked through this book and, I hope, found a speech that appeals to you, it is essential to get hold of the play text in order to understand the character as fully as you can. In some cases, it is best to look for a character who is no more than five years older or younger than you are yourself. Equally, don't choose a speech written in a different accent from your own unless you are very confident that you can pull it off.

Auditioning is a demanding process for everyone, and that includes those who are sitting in judgement: the directors, casting directors, producers, or examiners. If the audition is for a particular production, they know that a single mistake can doom their production to failure. Even the most brilliant director can't rescue a production that has been badly mis-cast. They are not only interested in choosing those who will be able to play the parts, but also those who will make a positive contribution to the rehearsal process. For the actors there is the fear of rejection. It's hardly surprising if, under the nervousness, many are furious that they have to put them-selves repeatedly through this ordeal. But Declan Donnellan, the artistic director of Cheek by Jowl, pointed out to me during research for this book that if auditions didn't exist, directors would repeatedly work with familiar faces, and the opportunities for new people would diminish.

An audition may be for a specific part, or with a view to joining a company putting on a number of plays, or it may be part of an exam, an entry requirement to a course, or a competition. In the first case you may also be required to read from the script. Some directors say that they have made up their minds within seconds of seeing the actor because they have a very clear idea of what they are looking for. Short of having plastic surgery, changing your genetic structure, or reliving your life, there's not a lot you can do about that. It may be that there's a part you could just make at a stretch, and the director is enthusiastic at the time; but there's always the possibility that someone else will come in later and hit the bull's eye. If you don't get the job there's no point in wasting time on wondering whether you were rejected be-cause you didn't smile at the right person, or because that witty riposte occurred to you on the tube going home rather than in the audition room.

There are, however, things you can do to help yourself prepare, apart from putting in as much work as possible on the speech. Give some thought to how you are going to dress, choosing clean and comfortable clothes, nothing too formal or too casual. Treat the audition as beginning from the moment you walk into the room. Most especially, prepare the introduction to the speech as well as the speech itself. Give the name of the play, the playwright and the context in which the character finds himself before the speech begins. If you don't do that, half of your audience's attention may be taken up with trying to work out what is going on rather than assessing your talent. Don't embarrass one person by addressing the entire speech to them. If the speech is to the audience, then embrace them all; if to an imaginary character or characters, take some time to establish where they are, to help the audience visualise them. If, after you have finished, the director chooses to work on the piece with you, then show that you are open to suggestion and aware that a piece may be played in many different ways. Above all, remember that auditioning makes everyone nervous, not just you. Don't try to fight it but rather – and this is easier said than done – try to use that nervous energy creatively instead. Good luck!

# Monologues for Women

# Baglady

FRANK MCGUINNESS

*First produced at the Peacock Theatre, Dublin, in 1985
with Maurean Toal as the Baglady.*

Walking incessantly by the river, babbling to herself, the Baglady is the kind of person you might well cross the road to avoid. But a fine actress, like Sorcha Cusack who played the part in London in 1988, can draw an audience into her story. Frank McGuinness's Irish monologue doesn't yield its secrets easily; rather, the audience has to listen hard and piece together the information that the Baglady lets slip. At first, she is aggressive as if we are the hostile yobs she inevitably encounters on the road, but gradually she takes us into her confidence. McGuinness describes her as wearing the heavy clothes of a farmer – rough trousers, dark overcoat and boots. Only a grey scarf completely hiding her hair suggests that she's a woman. She carries a grey, woollen sack like a burden on her back. Life on the road has aged her: she is much younger than she looks. What has reduced her to such a desperate state? In spite of her insistence that her father was 'a good man', it gradually becomes clear that she was abused by him as a child, that a baby was born and drowned in the river, and that the priest refused to believe her confession. She was given money to keep quiet but has spent it all in disgust. The combination of a guilty conscience, a secret to keep, and being treated as a liar has driven her close to madness. In spite of the Church's betrayal, her talk is suffused with Catholic imagery. All she has to eat and drink is white bread and red lemonade, which in this passage clearly remind her of communion. The play's intensity makes great demands on the actress.

# BAGLADY

*The Baglady walks.*

I can walk for miles without limping. I never stop. See my
hands, they make a bridge when I link them. Beneath the
link there's water running. I stand on the bridge and look
over. I see. I saw the river. It flowed beside our house. When
I stood beside the river, our house looked a long way away.
That's where I lived then, in our house, and my son lived in
the river. Sit down, I'll tell you about the house.

> *From her coat pocket the Baglady takes a slice of bread
> and a bottle of red lemonade. She sits, eating and
> drinking.*

We had electric in the house. Different colours in every room.
I liked red the best. The same colour as this lemonade. No,
red's never the same, no matter what way you look at it or
see where you see it. When you look into the sun, the red
blinds you. Blood can do that too, if you cut your head
badly. The electric light's a different red again. It was never
black when you put the red light on. You could see out
through the windows even in the night-time. And you could
see in. I used to breathe on the glass and write my mother's
name and my father's name on it. In the morning it was
never there, the names. The sun wiped them out. It was red
too. But you can't drink the sun nor blood nor the electric.
This is all I touch, red lemonade. All I eat, white bread.
I like the colours of them. You need money to buy the
colours. My father had money. Wads of it lying on the table
or smelling in his hands. Sometimes there was a picture of a
woman in his smell. She looked like a mad woman, dressed
all strangely, all in green. A green lady. I held her once in

my hands the only time I was trusted with money, because money's a man's responsibility. When you get married, make sure it's to a man who knows the value of money. If you don't, and you have money, give it away. Give it away, because money is a man's thing. Watch the way money moves to a man's hand. Pound notes, fivers, tenners, down on the table. I don't want it. It smells. Take it away from me. Keep away from me. I'll tell on you, I'll tell. We had electric in our house. It lit the whole room. I could see everything. I could see the money. I don't want it. Don't put out the light. Don't leave me in the black room. If I can't see, I can't talk, and if I can't talk, I can't tell. And I'm going to tell. I'm going to tell.

*The Baglady buries her face in her hands.*

# Been So Long

CHÉ WALKER

*First produced at the Royal Court Theatre Upstairs,
London, in 1998 with Sophie Okonedo as Simone.*

*Been So Long* by first-time playwright Ché Walker takes place
in the Bar Phoenix, a dying bar in Camden that can count its
customers on a single hand. It's a bar for losers; the winners
are across the road at Jakes, an MTV watering hole heaving
with young revellers who have come to Camden to enjoy a bit
of rough. The drinkers in the Phoenix pour out their feel-
ings to Barney the barman, who is content to observe life
from behind the counter. The play examines how men and
women relate to each other in a world in which you need to
be tough to survive. Raymond, who is pleasing to the eye, is
just out of jail and hoping to pick up a woman. He's fright-
ened he's lost his touch while inside. Simone and Yvonne, in
their late twenties, beautiful and scary, are regulars. Both
women have been hurt and are determined to use men like
Kleenex before they get abused again. But beneath the aggres-
sion, they are gooey romantics. Simone is a single mother
and has been deserted by her daughter's father. Her credo is:
'Never surrender, never concede, never forgive.' She and
Raymond spend the night together. She refuses to give him
her number but takes his. Although she's fallen for him, she
fails to get in touch, especially when she hears on the grape-
vine that he's been seeing another woman. In the speech
below, she and Raymond unexpectedly bump into each other
and he admits, 'You unpeeled me that night.' Their language
is an ornate, rhythmic mix of West Indian and London street
talk. She reveals to Raymond that she is not as hard-hearted
as she first appears, although that's a good reason not to get
involved, for she believes that Raymond, like so many men,

[7]

is incapable of being faithful: 'I'm getting dazzled in my belly, so this is where I get off.'

**Simone**  No. No. I'm sorry, Raymond, but you're the type a' geezer should come with a warning written on you. You're a child, Raymond.

You'll cut me up again. You're a charmer, and you did reach me, but this is not real, I don't trust it, you're runnin' round town fucking this girl and that, and already I'm hurt, and we're not even together, and I feel rejected and ugly and I'm thinkin' 'bout her and if you think she's nicer than me and better than me, and that's all I'm fucking thinking about since I heard, and I can't stop wantin' you and hearin' you and I resent them things, I resent it because I'm a proper big woman, Raymond, you understand me, I'm not fifteen, you understand me, and I'm subjugated already by wanting you so much, and yeah, you say you'll change but this is what you are, this is your meat and drink picking up birds and fucking with their heads just like this, I know all about this, Raymond, you get us hooked into your orbit and then you shit all over us, and I've been through this, this torture so many fucking times I swore that I'd never ask a man to give me pain again and I know from one good look at you that you can't stop, you don't have the strength to stop hurting women, and it cuts me because there really is something about you, darling, something I've seen and I really do think that I could love it, and I know it's the damage that locks you into doing all this bad stuff, I know that, but you scare me and I gotta go, Raymond, I'm sorry, but now I really must dust because looking at you makes me fifteen again, and I'm getting dazzled in my belly, so this is where I get off, I'm sorry because you're beautiful, and I'm gonna walk away now, Raymond . . .

# The Breath of Life

DAVID HARE

*First produced at the Theatre Royal, Haymarket, London, in 2002 with Judi Dench as Frances.*

Most unusually, *The Breath of Life* has two rewarding parts for women over sixty. More than that, they are not mad old crones living in the attic, but making their mark in the world today. No wonder David Hare's play attracted the interest of two theatrical Dames, Judi Dench and Maggie Smith, who came together onstage for the first time in decades. The women in the play once shared the same man, a radical lawyer called Martin, who later abandoned them both for a younger woman. Frances was the wife and Madeleine the mistress. The play describes a visit Frances pays to Madeleine's flat on the Isle of Wight. Ostensibly, Frances has come to talk to Madeleine because she wants to write her memoirs; since Martin's departure she has become a highly successful novelist of the 'Aga-saga' variety. Gradually, it becomes clear that what she really wants to do is to make some sense of her life. She is more conventional and needy than the acerbic and fiercely independent Madeleine. The two women, who have only met once fleetingly in the past, are in turn wary, hostile and humorous. Shortly after Frances arrives, she inexplicably drops off to sleep on the sofa – it's as if the strain of the visit overcomes her. When she wakes up it is evening, and the conversation becomes more intense. Madeleine describes how she first met Martin in Alabama, campaigning for civil rights in the sixties. This provokes Frances into describing what it was like living with Martin in the days following her discovery of his affair with Madeleine. Madeleine makes several interjections in the speech below, but because the memory is so acutely painful, Frances barely hears her.

**Frances** It was summer and we used to sit outside in the garden with a bottle of wine. He'd asked the vicar round. He'd met him in the street, he said, coming back from work. It was something he did. I'd noticed, he'd begun to do it quite often. I didn't quite get it . . .

It's not as if we'd ever been to church. Or knew the vicar, really. 'Vicar, what is the Church's current thinking on original sin?' And as this poor man began to answer, Martin would signal, he'd start signalling to me . . . sitting there, rolling his eyes, circling with his hand, as the vicar talked on.

*Frances imitates Martin's hand, revolving.*

'The vicar's lonely,' he used to say afterwards, after the second bottle. Sometimes a third. 'If we don't invite him, nobody will.' But even before that evening I'd realised: it's not the vicar who's lonely . . .

*Frances is regretful, remembering, before she goes on.*

'The Church's teaching on original sin,' he would say. 'You see, the thing that confuses me,' he would say – this was Martin, Martin would say, with a sort of relish, with a sense of fun, but also – I don't know, I think he also wanted to know. He would sit back in his chair, reach for his wine. 'Yours is such a *confusing* religion,' he would say . . . 'Man is born in sin, mired in sin, that's what your people say . . . But what does that mean? Tell me what that actually means,' he would say.

*Frances shakes her head.*

I remember that particular evening, sitting, watching, my wine in my hand, thinking: he's talking to the vicar. One hour ago he told me something. I asked and he told me. And now, what? There he is, sweet, untidy, slightly fat, slightly bald, Martin Beale QC, radical lawyer, talking to the vicar, grinning at me, circling with his hand, smiling, as if he and I are in some sort of conspiracy, as if, of course, he and I *understand* one another . . . and I? I don't even know . . . I'm so lost, I'm so bereft, I'm thinking: what do I want? I don't even know what I want.

*There is a pause.*

'Are we condemned to struggle, vicar, do we have no choice? And, tell me, vicar, is it written? Are we foredoomed to fail?' . . .

A couple of days later, as we're going upstairs, 'What was the orgy like?' I asked. 'Splendid,' he said. 'I wouldn't have missed it for the world.' . . .

I don't know . . . I really don't know. I was searching, I suppose, searching in him, for weeks, for months . . . like emptying an attic – what's that word? – *ransacking*, ransacking around inside Martin for a feeling. Looking all the time for a feeling . . .

*Suddenly Frances raises her voice, imitating Martin losing his temper.*

'What do you want, then? Tell me,' he said. 'What do you want? What do you fucking well want? That we go on living this life? In a fucking walled garden in Blackheath? Frances, are you serious? Nothing to our lives except that?'

*Frances becomes quieter.*

'And what if I'm hurt? What if it hurts, what you've told me?' He looked at me. 'Well then, you're hurt.'

*There's a silence.*

Days of thinking, 'Oh this is fine. I can handle this.' Then, 'Are you still seeing her?' 'Well, I am, if that's OK with you.' 'Well, it's not OK with me.' 'Well, it's what I'm going to do.' Then a long silence, a long, long silence, maybe thirty minutes or more. Maybe an hour. Then me getting up. 'Well, if it's what you're going to do, why fucking ask? Why fucking ask?'

# The Country

MARTIN CRIMP

*First produced at the Royal Court Theatre, London, in 2000 with Indira Varma as Rebecca.*

Martin Crimp's oblique, chilling, short play concerns a doctor, his wife and his mistress. Information about these people is only slowly leaked out to the audience. The doctor, Richard, and his wife, Corinne, have recently moved to the Fells. The country is first seen as a place of retreat from the city – there are references to Virgil – where it is possible to sit under a tree by a stream for a whole afternoon enjoying the view. Later, it proves to be a false haven. In Vicki Mortimer's original design, the forest loomed over the room in which the play is set.

At the beginning of the play, Richard brings Rebecca, an academic, back to their house, claiming that he found her collapsed by the roadside. Corinne at first seems unreasonably suspicious, wondering whether he would have done the same if it had been an old drunk by the road instead of a beautiful young woman. She's alarmed when she discovers needles in Rebecca's handbag, for she knows that her husband has used drugs illegally in the city and begins to suspect his involvement in Rebecca's collapse. Richard is reluctantly forced to go out on a call, leaving the two women together. Rebecca awakes and they have a hostile, pedantic discussion about the meaning of certain words. Rebecca is the intruder, more powerful in that she knows more about Corinne than Corinne does about her. . Rebecca reveals that Richard came to the Fells in order to pursue her. They had been having a damaging, obsessive affair from which she had tried to escape. Having heard this news, Corinne leaves the house with the children, while Rebecca waits for Richard to return. When he does, Rebecca doesn't tell him that they are alone. Instead, she makes a series of requests that are refused because Richard is afraid of a confrontation. Most of all she wants to see the children. She then imagines telling them a bedtime story in which she describes how she and Richard met. The words 'medicine' and 'treatment' take on a sinister overtone. Her story depicts a disturbing distortion of a doctor's healing role.

**Rebecca**  But everyone wants to hear a story, don't they?
I could say: Hello. I'm Rebecca. I'm the maid. Let me tell
you a story. Would you like me to tell you a story? Oh yes
please, Rebecca, tell us a story. Well once upon a time,
children, there was a girl, there was a bright young girl,
and she was sick, and she needed some medicine. So she
went to a doctor and she said: Doctor, doctor, it hurts,
I need some medicine. But the doctor wouldn't give her
any. He said, go away – don't waste my time – I have no
medicine. So she went back again and she said: Doctor,
doctor, it really hurts, I need some medicine. And this time
the doctor went to the door. He locked the door. He said:
I need to take a history – roll up your sleeve. So she rolled
up her sleeve and the doctor took a history. Then, children,
he got one instrument to look into her eyes. And another
instrument to listen to her heart. And when he'd looked
into her eyes and listened to her heart, he asked her to
undress.

And when she'd undressed, he said: I see now how very
sick you are – you need some medicine. She said: Doctor,
am I going to die? He said: No, it's simply that your eyes
are very dark and your skin is very pale. Your skin is so
thin that when I touch it like this with my lips I can feel the
blood moving underneath. You're sick, that's all. You need
some medicine. So the treatment began.

The treatment was wild, children. It could take place at
any time of day or night. In any part of the city. In any part
of her body. Her body . . . became the city. The doctor
learned how to unfold her – like a map.

Until one day the bright young girl decided the treatment
would have to end – because the more medicine she took,

the more medicine she craved – and besides, she was leaving for the country.

Now this made the doctor very angry. Because he'd broken all the rules – as he saw it – for her. Not just the kind of rules you children have – take off your shoes, wash your hands – but grown-up rules. Laws. He'd broken all these rules – these laws – and he was very angry. In fact he wept. You bitch, he said. You little bitch.

Because you see there'd been a terrible misunderstanding. Since the thing the bright young girl bitch called treatment, the doctor – who of course was sick himself – who craved medicine himself – imagined to be – what? – something personal. Something human. Which is why he followed her.

# Decadence

## STEVEN BERKOFF

*First produced at the New End Theatre, London, in 1981
with Linda Marlowe as Helen.*

Steven Berkoff has written in his autobiography: 'Many
actors find that they can identify with my works and like to
test themselves out in auditions. The irony is that the compa-
nies for whom they audition wouldn't dream of having a
Berkoff play in their repertoire, but they have to listen to all
those Berkovian speeches. Forced to. Oh Bliss.' He's right in
that his plays are crammed with vivid speeches suitable for
auditions. Here's one on which you can test yourself. In
*Decadence*, Berkoff demands a physical performance style to
match the torrent of profane, rhythmic language. No realism
here. Two actors each play two parts: the upper-class Helen
and Steve, who can't keep their hands off each other; and the
lower-class Sybil, who is married to Steve and has hired a
private detective, Les, to spy on her husband. Together, Helen
and Steve wallow in all the excesses of the eighties, revelling
in their lust and gluttony. The part of Helen is written to be
performed in the strangulated vowel tones of the upper
classes. Berkoff describes the type in his introduction to the
play: 'They move in awkward rapid gestures or quick jerks
and sometimes speak at rapid speeds to avoid appearing to
have any feeling for what they say. They achieve pleasure very
often in direct relation to the pain they cause in achieving it.'

As Steve and Helen prepare to go out for the evening,
Helen describes riding to the hunt – performed onstage with
Steve between her legs – in which the combination of the feel
of the horse beneath her, the thrill of the chase and the fox's
death drive her into an orgasmic ecstasy.

# DECADENCE

**Helen**  The morning hung crisp over the village like a Chanel voile gown or a bouclé ruffle / hunting is so fucking thrilling / if you haven't done it / it's like explaining a fuck to the pope / do you know what I mean? it's the togetherness / the meeting at the morning pub / the stomp of horses and that lovely bloody smell / the preparation, pulling those fucking jodhpurs on / bloody hell they can be tight after a binge the previous night hello Claude and what ho Cecil! There's Jeremiah and Quentin / Jennifer / Vanessa darling you do look fab / that jacket fits you like a glove / the asses of the men look small and pretty bouncing on their steaming steeds / snorting from their sculptured snouts / what a sight / off we go, we shout / the leader of the hounds sounds his horn / they're straining hard 'gainst the curbing leash / a pack of hate / bursting to get free / dying to get that nasty little beast / yoiks and tally ho and onwards we shall go / the bloody fox let loose he scampers out all keenly in the bush / he has a bloody good time / a jolly taste of pure excitement / who doesn't like a smashing race? / The leader sounds the horn the scent's been picked up / dashed good form / heels dig in ribs the horses swing to face the direction of the horn's sweet ring / on we go over hill and dale / watching for the bloody foxy fox's tail / gosh Cynthia's fallen in the muck / bloody bad luck! / over the brook / dash over the stream / my pounding steed's just one with me / it's hard / the saddle chafes / it's tough / my pussy feels delightful though with each successive thrilling dash / it heaves up huge between my thighs / this hot and heaving sweating beast / it tugs my hips / it heaves me on / on to the golden hills of Acheron / I grip him hard / my knees dig in I soar up high / I float / I flow / I'm thrown into the sky and then thud down / the air is singed in smells of mud / crushed grass / horse shit and sweat / mixed up in one divine and bloody mess / we've lorst the fucker / oh bloody balls the nag's confused / the scent is lorst / the dogs go searching / now confused / now whining / now all cross / oh shit and piss! The fucking league of love the bloody foxes sabotaged the scent! / The careful thread, the ribbon of fear that leads us on to the bloody kill / those left-wing bastards jealous as hell / to see their betters enjoying themselves / threw scent to confuse / those rotten sods / I'd thrash them black and blue I'd have them flogged / those dirty, poofy, Marxist, working-class yobs / wait! Pluto's found the scent again! Oh fab. We're off! Tarquin bloodies one of their noses! Oh heavens, it's just raining roses / he's on the ground and Tarquin's ready to drive his horse into the bugger / Jeremy says nay / restrains hot Tarquin / they'll come another day! He says / Oh bravo! Dashing! Super! Wow! I'm going now / look at meeeeeee! / The day's spun rich in magenta to auburn / the hounds shriek louder / the scent grows strong / the fox is tired / my cheeks are red / my eyes are bright / blood will be shed / oh god it's getting fucking awful thrilling / the flesh is weak but the spirit is willing / my pants have come galore / and my ass is deliciously bloody sore / we're close / the fox has gone to ground / we'll find the little beastly hound / yes! It's trapped down in some gully / horses crash through the farmer's land / all in a hurry / tear up the crops / oh dear / we'll pay later never fear / oh fuck! Some kid's pet cat is torn to shreds in the wake of the enthusiastic chase / never mind there's plenty more / ah, we've got him now / I see it caught / it's trapped / its breath is pounding out in horrible short stabs / its fear setting each hair on end / the hounds all teeth and smiles as they go in and sink their fangs into its throat / the blood was one long jet / just fabulous / I'm sure the fox was pleased to make his end this way / the fury / the chase / the ecstasy / the embrace / the leader dismounts / cuts off its tail /

bloodies the kids / oh they were thrilled / oh what a day /
let's have a gin and tonic / whadya say / lovely life /
wouldn't have it any other way.

# The Fastest Clock in the Universe

PHILIP RIDLEY

*First produced at Hampstead Theatre, London, in 1992
with Emma Amos as Sherbet.*

The Fastest Clock in the Universe won a clutch of awards
when it was first performed. Ridley's location is typically
gothic, the names of the characters exotic and the plot re-
sembles a nightmare. Cougar Glass and Captain Tock live in
a claustrophobic room with cracks in the walls above a fur
factory where the animals used to be skinned alive. Cougar
is the dominant partner and treats the Captain as if he were
scum. When the play opens, preparations are in hand for
Cougar's nineteenth birthday party, a landmark he has celeb-
rated many times before. In fact, he is thirty and obsessed
with the passing of time and the fading of his looks. His hair
is jet-black and roughly styled in a quiff. Only one guest is
invited to this party, the good-looking Foxtrot Darling, whom
Cougar plans to seduce. The Captain has his orders to leave
as soon as Cougar gives the word. Disaster strikes when
Foxtrot (played by Jude Law in the original production)
arrives bringing Sherbet with him and announces that he is
engaged to her. She further informs Cougar and the Captain
that she is pregnant with Foxtrot's child. Sherbet is only
sixteen years old, described by Ridley as having 'long curly
red hair and lots of glamorous make-up. She is wearing a
white uniform, stilettos and clutching a handbag covered in
pink sequins.' Cougar sulks in the background while Sherbet
takes control, producing party hats out of her bag, and
mocking Cougar's refusal to join in the party games. She
treats him like a sulky child. In contrast with the outlandish
setting, Sherbet makes a point of declaring her love for all
things traditional. There is a fierce battle between Cougar

and Sherbet for Foxtrot's affections, in which both of them are prepared to play dirty. This speech is one of the first indications that Sherbet has expertly deduced exactly how old Cougar is and is biding her time before spilling the beans.

**Sherbet** I wish to grow old gracefully. Now I know that sounds ridiculous, but I've seen enough people not doing it gracefully to know what I'm talking about. The beauty salon where I work is full of them. Men and women. All with the same look in their eyes. Make me young, says the look. But you know something? There's nothing we can do. Nature has rules and regulations and most of them are either cruel or fucking cruel. You know, I can usually tell a person's age as easy as that! One look is all it takes. Fancy that, Cougar, eh?

*Cougar backs away.*

There's this one woman who comes in – I feel sorry for her in a way – and she's got this photograph of what she looked like when she was nineteen. She must be sixty if she's a bloody day now. Anyway, she comes in and she shows me this photo and – fucking hell! – was she beautiful! 'This was me,' she says. It's as if that photograph captured her at the happiest moment of her life. Perhaps it's like that. Perhaps we reach our peak when we're nineteen and, for one glorious summer, we're in control of our lives, and we look wonderful and everything is perfect. And then it's never the same again. And we spend the rest of our lives merely surviving one empty summer after another.

# Frozen

BRYONY LAVERY

*First produced at the Birmingham Repertory Theatre in 1998, then at the National Theatre, London, in 2002 with Anita Dobson as Nancy.*

In *Frozen*, Nancy sends her ten-year-old daughter round to her grandma's with a pair of secateurs and never sees her again. Who would want to see a play on such a topic? But although the subject is almost unbearable, Bryony Lavery, unlike many in the media, scrupulously avoids both sensationalism and sentimentality. Her integrity is never in question. *Frozen* has just three characters, who speak as much to the audience as to each other: Nancy; Ralph, the serial killer who only cares for his videos with titles such as *Lollitots* and *Lesbian Lolita*; and Agnetha, the American psychiatrist who is exploring the theory that many serial killers have been brain-damaged through abuse in their childhood and are ill rather than sinners. All three are in an emotional deep freeze. The play covers over twenty years from the disappearance of Rhona to Ralph's suicide. To begin with, Nancy, a deeply conventional woman, describes her efforts to cope with the teenage war zone. Anita Dobson, who first played Nancy, adopted a bright girlish voice that perfectly reflected the carapace with which the mother surrounds herself immediately after Rhona disappears. She starts an organisation to search for missing children and tirelessly tours the country to publicise the cause. Her false optimism and energy begin to crack in the speech below – an emotional turning point in the play – as she describes the day the police came to inform her, twenty years after Rhona had disappeared, that they had found her skeleton nearby. Then Nancy has all the expected reactions of grief,

anger and a desperate desire for revenge. Eventually she for-
gives Ralph, but in her own time.

# FROZEN

*Nancy walking, three or four days later.*

**Nancy**
   Sun's so hot.

   Four days ago
   phone call from the police
   they think they have some news for us
   can they come over?

   Terrible terrible restlessness anxiety
   then two young policemen . . . *lads* . . .
   one with fine soft hair like a kiddie's . . .
   other lovely polished shoes
   pitch up
   say . . .
   'We have apprehended a man in the
   unsuccessful attempted abduction of a young girl . . .
   subsequent inquiries have uncovered a lock-up shed
   the earth floor contains the remains of other children
   the man is now giving us names
   one of them'

   he says

   'is Rhona.'

*Sound of great ice floes breaking up, cracking, churning.*

   I wanted to go out for a walk
   up a hill somewhere

   find some fresh air
   there's no air.

Message
after message
after message
on the answerphone.
Newspapers
we must we must we must
want to talk to them.

Ingrid rings
comes over
makes something with noodles
can't touch it
but I show willing
twirl it around on the plate a bit with a fork.
Ingrid says
'Try with chopsticks . . . I'll show you how to . . .'
but I leave it all sitting there
dumped on the plate

puts me in mind of worms

I've given Bob some more paracetamol
his headache's approaching Gale Force . . .

All this time
I've been growing her up
she's been
he's had her buried away . . .

I wish this weather would break.

I wish it would pour it down.
It's unbearable.

Great Big Storm.

*A huge storm breaks . . .*

# In Flame

CHARLOTTE JONES

*First produced at the Bush, London, in 1999 with Valerie
Gogan as Alex; then at the New Ambassadors Theatre,
London, with Kerry Fox as Alex.*

The emphasis of Charlotte Jones's warm and funny play is on
the plight of its female characters, some living at the end and
others at the beginning of the twentieth century. Bad things
happen to these women, but male critics were oversensitive
in feeling that their sex was under attack when the play was
first seen at the Bush. Jones is rather suggesting that, although
womens' lives have improved over the century, relationships
of all kinds are always potentially painful and that women
are invariably burdened with guilt. In 1908 in Yorkshire,
Livvy is seduced by a fairground photographer who aban-
dons her. In disgrace, she is about to be forced into marrying
a doltish butcher she doesn't love when she dies from an
ectopic pregnancy. Alex, on the other hand, should be the
epitome of what women can achieve at the end of the twen-
tieth century. In fact, she is a thirty-six-year-old cartographer
who has lost her way. She feels guilty about putting her
mother, Annie, into a home; her best friend is jealous of her;
and her rich, married lover, with whom she has amazing sex,
refuses to leave his wife. Her senile mother is the unreliable
link between her and Livvy, whose photograph Alex has found.
Annie is especially stroppy with Alex, often pretending not
to recognise her. Alex believes it's because she and her father
used to gang up against her when Alex was young – something
else for the daughter to feel guilty about. In Alex's speech
below, she visits her mother in hospital on her birthday.
Annie's ancestors are calling her to leave this world; Livvy,
who speaks to the old woman, cannot be seen nor heard by

[ 35 ]

Alex. Time is running out for the mother and daughter to make their peace.

*The nursing home.*

**Alex**  Here we are then, Mother.

*She gets the tap shoes out and places them before her.*

Nothing to hold you back now. And I've brought you
another treat. Raspberry Royale. That's what you wanted,
isn't it? They had Sherry Trifle too but you turned your
nose up at that last time. Ah. We're going for the silent
treatment, are we?

*Pause. The next is very chatty, light, conversational.*

Well. It's my birthday today. I didn't get your card. Second
post, maybe. Thirty-six today. I don't look it? Thank you
very much. I use extremely expensive eye cream. Guaranteed
to cover that 'not-quite-as-fertile-as-I-used-to-be look' that's
creeping up under my eyes. Anyway, I'm meeting Mat later.
Did I tell you about him? I don't think you'd approve. He's
an acquired taste. And he's married. I fell right into that
cliché. Very good in bed, though. We get up to all sorts.
Your mind, if you had one, would boggle. He never holds
my feet though . . .

*Pause.*

Come on, tuck in. Can't let a good Raspberry Royale go
to waste. Raspberries fit for a queen. Come on. You don't
have to watch your figure any more. Open wide and let the
choo-choo train in.

*Pause. The tone is sharper suddenly.*

Eat up, Mother. It's a treat. Come on.

*She feeds her during the next.*

Oh dear, it's all down your front, Mother. You look a right old mess, don't you?

*She looks at her.*

You're very quiet today. Now you haven't got your audience . . . But I can see you're thinking. It's all going on in there, isn't it? Pickfords must have been, Mother. The careful movers. Packed you away with the crocks and the glassware. But it's all right because I know what you're thinking. Slugs leave trails, you see.

*Alex comes right up close to her.*

I was a little girl. You were the one who turned it into a competition. I was just a little girl. Sweetness and light, my arse. You play dirty, don't you, Anne? . . .

Well it doesn't matter. He's dead now. My dad's dead. I still dream about him, though. It's a recurring dream. We're at Weston-super-Mare and we're burying you in the sand. And then we just leave you. We run off together and we have ice cream. Neopolitan flavour, because I can never choose. And I wake up and I feel safe and then I realise that we've forgotten you, you're still there buried in the sand and I feel guilty for the rest of the day . . .

What's so ironic, what you don't realise, Ma, is I still want to help you. I'm here with my spade. And I'm ready to dig . . .

But you're not interested, are you? . . .

Just answer me one thing, Mother, why does this feel like a punishment? You being ill, and helpless. Tell me what I've done. Come on.

*Alex sighs.*

Well, you win.

*As an afterthought she kisses her on the head.*

*She leaves.*

# The Late Middle Classes

SIMON GRAY

*First produced at the Palace Theatre, Watford, in 1999
with Harriet Walter as Celia.*

Simon Gray's autobiographical play is about betrayal, hypo-
crisy and the emotional repressions of the 1950s. A young
boy, Holly, is caught between his snobbish, protective, anti-
Semitic parents, and his Austrian piano teacher and composer,
a closet homosexual who is treated like an alien in the small
community that lives on an island close to the Isle of Wight.
The play is often distressing, but this is a comic speech close
to the beginning in which Celia, Holly's mother, reveals the
frustrations of returning to domestic life after the responsi-
bilities of driving an ambulance during the war. Her days are
filled with drinking gin, playing tennis and tracking down
food, which *was* still rationed. She is a lively, glamorous but
also superficial woman married to a pathologist. Their marri-
age is ostensibly happy, but Celia looks to Holly rather than
her husband to give her the love she needs. She is desperate
that he should win a scholarship to either Westminster or St
Paul's in order that they can move to London and away from
the island she finds so dull. Celia bickers with her son before
she makes this phone call, and her boredom is so intense that
afterwards, in one of her many self-dramatising moments,
she pretends to be dead, to the alarm of the poor boy. The
reference to 'Winnie' is to Winston Churchill.

**Celia** (*on telephone*) Oh, Bunty dear, it's Celia. It just struck me, lovely afternoon, a bit of a breeze, what do you say to a game of tennis?

*Little pause.*

Well, right now really. I mean, as soon as we've changed. We can be at the court in ten minutes – oh, don't be so silly, dear, you're a very good *natural* player, all you need is practice – and weight has nothing to do with it, many marvellous players are as heavy as you – what? No, no, I don't mean that at all, all I mean is something you said the other day about being worried that you're getting a little – a little – and what better way to get it off?

*Pause.*

Oh, very well, dear, if you really feel I'm inviting you to join a chain gang instead of a mild knock-up – what? Moira? No, no, she's a bit under the weather, she says, and anyway I don't fancy an hour with Moira, all she'll talk about is how marvellous everything is and their wretched holiday in Ireland with all the steaks and butter and fresh cream. Which reminds me, my dear, have you got any eggs from those chickens of yours, I want to give Charles a surprise, he was saying last night how much he yearned for an omelette, but with fresh eggs, not powdered – oh – oh, well never mind, Bunty dear, I was going to offer you some chocolate in exchange but I expect that the last thing you want at the moment is chocolate so it'll have to be dried eggs again, they'll just have to put up with it – what? Wait? Oh, some-body at the door – somebody at the window? Oh, tapping on the window – well, I really haven't got anything more to –

*Stands, waiting, lights another cigarette, taps her foot irritably.*

Who is it? Moira! Tapping on your window! What does she want? A cup of tea! Moira taps on your window whenever she wants a cup of tea – no, no, thank you, dear, really what I want to be is outside, you see. Give Moira my – my –

*She hangs up.*

Really, these people – these people on this bloody island, I don't know how I put up with them. Always presuming on one's friendship. If they didn't claim to be friends they wouldn't dare to do the kind of thing they do do. Of course it's easy for them, they've both got help, they can play tennis or have their cups of tea with each other whenever they like. While I – what on earth was the point of our winning the war if you end up worse off than before it started? No housekeeper, no maid, while both of them have got both. And Bunty's even got a gardener. Well, she calls him a gardener but really he looks like a convict – pasty-faced and furtive and smoking, and doesn't even know how to say good morning. Doesn't speak at all as far as I know. He may be one of those Eyetie prisoners of war who stayed on. But if you've got an Italian prisoner of war in your garden I suppose you do feel you've won the war and everything's almost back to normal. In spite of Winnie being thrown out.

# Medea Redux

NEIL LABUTE

*First produced at the Douglas Fairbanks Theatre, New York City, in 1999 with Mary McCormack as the Woman.*

The Greek tragedies cast their shadow over Neil LaBute's *Bash*, a trilogy of short plays of which *Medea Redux* is one of two monologues. The title alone suggests that you're not in for a light evening. Euripides' play describes how Medea takes her revenge on Jason, the man she once helped to steal the Golden Fleece from her family. When Jason announces that he is abandoning her for another woman, Medea murders their children in a terrible act of vengeance. How could a mother do such a thing?

The character in LaBute's monologue is no queen of the past, but rather a desperate, under-educated, institutionalised American woman of today, sitting under a harsh light and making a statement into a tape recorder. She smokes and fiddles with a cup of water throughout. Her story is pitiful but she never asks for pity. She describes how at thirteen she was seduced by a teacher she had always admired. He takes her on excursions, tells her about the Greeks, and introduces her to Billie Holiday. When she discovers she's pregnant, she promises her lover that she will never give his name away. Even so, he flees – a fact she only discovers by accident – and she is left to bring up her son alone. Many years later, they agree to meet up on the boy's fourteenth birthday in Arizona. The father is now married but has had no more children. A smug, triumphant grin on his face as he leans over to kiss his son seals the boy's fate. As he has shown in his film *In the Company of Men*, LaBute is never afraid of looking at the dark side of male behaviour. Here the girl is both a victim and also responsible for a horrendous act. In this passage,

[ 43 ]

she describes how she went to see her teacher to tell him she was pregnant.

i, umm . . . found out about the baby, that i was going to have one, in late april, the 23rd, i guess, and i didn't cry. i should've, fucking kid myself, you know, but sometimes you can go along, years even, and not feel like you're growing up at all, and then there's times when you age a ton, like, in a couple a' seconds. you know? so, i found out and went straight to his place, i mean, called first, but went there and we discussed it all. talked a long time . . . (*Beat.*) we talked, like i said, and, you know, he seemed, and this caught me, 'cause i didn't know what he'd think, but he was all excited! not yelling, or all adult and shit, and said he loved children, could think of nothing better than having a son or something. said we'd have to be careful – i mean, we both understood the situation – but i promised him i wouldn't tell anybody who the father was, no matter if my dad got really shitty about it – and he did, believe me – or school, or whatever. i said i'd keep our secret . . . we made a pledge together, there on his sofa, and i kept it. (*Beat.*) he told me that day, he said he had to go away for a couple weeks, just the end of summer, he was finishing up another of his degrees at delphi, that's a university, and then we'd, you know, make some plans. (*Beat.*) that was hard, 'cause i was scared, i'm not gonna pretend i wasn't, but getting his degree was a big thing, and could help us, too, he said . . . and so we talked for a while, and we kissed. god, you know for being this big guy, he was really gentle to me . . . and then i went home. i went to my house with our baby inside me, and watched *hogan's heroes* on tv, like i did every afternoon. i mean, what else are you gonna do, right? (*Beat.*) i just need a little water . . .

    *She pours a touch more into her cup and sips.*

ok. umm, what else? ahh . . . when i found out he'd left his position at school – this was by a fluke, anyway – i was at the general office during the summer, which was not that far from our house, bringing them a vaccination report on my brother, and the lady there, the secretary, said, 'oh, i heard about your arts and sciences teacher at gardner,' my school, 'we're sure sorry to lose him, aren't we?'– i didn't hear much else, really, just that she said, 'well, i suppose they need good teachers in phoenix as much as they do anywhere . . .' (*Beat.*) but i didn't ask for an address or anything, i didn't, because i was standing there, in that office, suddenly standing there, fourteen years old with a baby in me and this woman yacking on about my brother needing a german measles booster, and did i know if he'd had one yet, and i was frozen in time. 's like the heavens had opened above me, at that very second, and all i could hear was the universe. this woman in front of me talking on like i was her godchild and all i could make out was the howl of the cosmos . . . and you know what? it was laughing. it was. all its attention was suddenly turned and it was laughing, laughing down at me . . .

*She stops and slowly lights another cigarette.*

# The Mercy Seat

NEIL LABUTE

*First produced at the Manhattan Class Company (MCC) Theater, New York City, in 2002 with Sigourney Weaver as Abby Prescott.*

Neil LaBute's play is set on 12 September 2001, the day after the attack on the World Trade Center. A layer of dust covers the expensive furniture in Abby's loft apartment and an amber haze hangs in the air. Abby is a decisive, dynamic executive in her forties who is frustrated by her lover's inability to decide whether or not to ring his wife and let her know he's survived. Ben probably owes his life to the fact that he stopped off to see Abby on his way to the World Trade Center. While the scale of the tragedy appals her, he is seized by the idea that the attack is an opportunity, a chance for them to run away together, deceiving his family into thinking he was killed. Abby is Ben's boss and twelve years older. After three years of keeping their affair a secret, she yearns to live with him, but Ben has always failed to find the courage to leave his wife. Being more intelligent than him, Abby knows that his plan stinks. Apart from its illegality, the strain of abandoning his children – he would never be able to see them again – would be bound to poison their life together. She is also appalled by his determination to exploit a national tragedy for his own ends. During a long night of the soul, which is reminiscent of *Who's Afraid of Virginia Woolf?* (although without the booze), their rawest feelings are exposed, from Abby's concern that she's guilty of sexual harassment to Ben's fury when she mocks his inarticulacy. He feels patronised, especially when she laughs at him for failing to pick up on her cultural references. In the following passage, Abby decides to go for broke and the truth-telling gets dangerously close to the bone.

**Abby** It's funny, I probably shouldn't even go there, but – it's comical, almost . . . almost comical the things you can imagine while you're making love that way. Face down. Turned away from a person. It is to me, anyway. The ideas, or images, or, you know, just *stuff* . . . that goes through your head if you do it that way for too long. Ha! Wow, it's . . . I don't know. Just funny . . .

Things that you'd never expect, or be prepared for, or anything; visions that will just suddenly appear as you're kneeling there. Doing it. Having it done to you. 'Cause that's what it's like when you have sex that way all the time, like it's being done to you. That it really doesn't matter to the person back there who 'it' is. Just that it – meaning, a backside – is there and available and willing. And so a lot of the time when you're going at it, my mind has just drifted off and I'll think such crazy thoughts . . . sometimes fantasies, like it's somebody else, a lover I've taken, or that I'm being attacked, jumped in an alleyway by some person . . . or I'll just make lists, 'to do' lists for work or shopping or whatnot. I can remember figuring out all my Christmas ideas one night in Orlando at the Hyatt there, during one of our little . . . on the carpet, as I recall. . . do you remember that night? We had those adjoining suites. . . that was a nice conference. In fact, that might've been where I first noticed your particular bent for . . . well, you know. My *back porch* . . .

But most of the time I just imagine that it's your wife. Lately that's the thought that I can't seem to get out of my head. That it's your sweet little Mrs from the suburbs behind me with one of those, umm, things – those, like, *strappy* things that you buy at sex shops – and she's just going to town on me. Banging away for hours because of what I've done to her life, and you know what? I let her. I let her do it, because somewhere inside I feel like I probably deserve it, it's true . . . and when I think about it, when I stop and really take it in for a moment, it doesn't actually feel that much different than when we do it. Honestly. I mean, in some ways, who better? She knows what you do it like, the speed, rhythm, all that. Unless you do it with her all pretty and tender and who knows what. Do you? No, probably not . . . she's probably read the ol' *mattress tag* more times than even me, God bless 'er. (*Beat.*) I dunno. Maybe that's what Hell is, in the end. All of your wrongful shit played out there in front of you while you're being pumped from behind by someone you've hurt. That you've screwed over in life. Or worse, worse still . . . some person who doesn't really love you any more. No one to ever look at again, make contact with. Just you being fucked as your life splashes out across this big headboard in the devil's bedroom. Maybe. Even if that's not it, even if Hell is all fire and sulphur and that sort of thing, it couldn't be much worse than that.

# Night and Day

TOM STOPPARD

*First produced at the Phoenix Theatre, London, in 1978
with Diana Rigg as Ruth.*

Tom Stoppard's *Night and Day* is a polemical piece which is
very much a play of its time, partly because the battles bet-
ween the press barons and union closed shops were then at
their height, but also because the plot hinges on the crucial
importance of a telex machine – a telex was then one of the
few ways of getting information out in a hurry – in a fictional
African country threatened with civil war. Stoppard explores
the idea of press freedom through the two characters of
Milne, an idealistic, provincial journalist who is blackballed
by the unions because he won't join a strike over parity pay,
and Dick Wagner, a hard-drinking union man, proud to be a
hack and ruthless in his pursuit of a story. They are both
working for the *Sunday Globe* – Milne as a freelancer – and
are both observed by Ruth, the intelligent, sardonic and sophis-
ticated wife of Geoffrey, the mining engineer who owns the
telex. Her opinion of the press has been personally soured by
the circumstances of her divorce in which she, her new hus-
band, and his ex-wife were pursued by Fleet Street's finest.
Most of all she can't reconcile the ideal of press freedom with
the content, summed up by such headlines as 'Beauty Queen
in Tug-of-Love Baby Storm'. 'I'm with you on the free press,'
she tells Milne. 'It's the newspapers I can't stand.' She's not
quite as cynical as the African leader who describes a rela-
tively free press as a press run by one of his relatives.

Ruth, who is in her late thirties, is lacking in freedom
herself. She is no more than fond of her husband and feels
herself both isolated and trapped in Africa. She is also guil-
tily attracted to Milne, who is later killed on a dangerous

mission to meet the rebel leader. Ruth is distressed by his death but also appalled that a man's life has been wasted, dying for the cause of trying to fill space in a newspaper. George is a photographer working with the journalists.

**Ruth** (*with the paper*) This thing that's worth dying for . . .
Show me where it is. It can't be on the back page – 'Rain
Halts Australian Collapse.' That's not it, is it? Or the
woman's page – 'Sexy Or Sexist? – The Case for Intimate
Deodorants.' Is that it, George? What about readers'
letters? – 'Dear Sir, If the Prime Minister had to travel on
the seven fifty-three from Bexhill every morning we'd soon
have the railwaymen back on the lines.' Am I getting warm,
George? . . .

(*angrily*) You bet I am. I'm not going to let you think he
died for free speech and the guttering candle of democracy –
crap! You're all doing it to impress each other and be top
dog the next time you're propping up a bar in Beirut or
Bangkok, or Chancery Lane. Look at Dick and tell me I'm
a liar. He's going to be a hero. The wires from London are
going to burn up with congratulations. They'll be talking
about Wagner's scoop for years, or anyway Wagner will.
It's all bloody ego. And the winner isn't democracy, it's
just business. As far as I'm concerned, Jake died for the
product. He died for the women's page, and the crossword,
and the racing results, and the heartbreak beauty queens
and somewhere at the end of a long list I suppose he died
for the leading article too, but it's never worth *that* –

*She has started to swipe at Guthrie with a newspaper
and she ends up flinging it at him.*

# Old Times

## HAROLD PINTER

*First produced by the Royal Shakespeare Company at the Aldwych Theatre, London, in 1971 with Dorothy Tutin as Kate.*

Harold Pinter's *Old Times* has many speeches that could be used for auditions, some of which give a lively picture of the concert halls, pubs, cafés and parties enjoyed by two secretaries, Kate and Anna, flat-sharing in London in the late forties and early fifties. The play, however, is set somewhere on the coast in England, a quiet retreat where Kate now lives with her husband Deeley. They are waiting for Anna to pay them a visit. Deeley has never met Anna before and is unaware of just how close the two women used to be. When Anna arrives, Deeley quickly becomes jealous of her intimate knowledge of his wife's past. Kate, who is more passive and dreamy than the others, observes that they talk about her as if she were dead.

Both Deeley and Anna use their memories of the past, often contradictory, in order to score points over the other. As Anna says: 'There are some things one remembers even though they may never have happened. There are things I remember which may never have happened but as I recall them so they take place.' Deeley describes how he first met Kate when he picked her up coming out of a fleapit having just seen the film *Odd Man Out*. He describes how they were the only two people in the cinema. Anna contends later that she and Kate went to see the same film together. Deeley becomes coarser and more absurd as his desperation increases. He is clearly imagining that Anna and Kate had an affair together. He tries to diminish Anna by claiming that he remembers seeing her at a party and looking up her skirt. It is only when

Deeley seems completely defeated that Kate finally asserts herself. She describes the moment at which her affection for Anna died. She talks of how she brought a man, possibly Deeley, back to their room and how they lay on Anna's bed, and how she denied that anyone had slept there before him. 'No one at all' are the chilling last words of the play.

**Kate** (*to Anna*) But I remember you. I remember you dead.

   *Pause.*

I remember you lying dead. You didn't know I was watching you. I leaned over you. Your face was dirty. You lay dead, your face scrawled with dirt, all kinds of earnest inscriptions, but unblotted, so that they had run, all over your face, down to your throat. Your sheets were immaculate. I was glad. I would have been unhappy if your corpse had lain in an unwholesome sheet. It would have been graceless. I mean as far as I was concerned. As far as my room was concerned. After all, you were dead in my room. When you woke my eyes were above you, staring down at you. You tried to do my little trick, one of my tricks you had borrowed, my little slow smile, my little slow shy smile, my bend of the head, my half-closing of the eyes, that we knew so well, but it didn't work, the grin only split the dirt at the sides of your mouth and stuck. You stuck in your grin. I looked for tears but could see none. Your pupils weren't in your eyes. Your bones were breaking through your face. But all was serene. There was no suffering. It had all happened elsewhere. Last rites I did not feel necessary. Or any celebration. I felt the time and season appropriate and that by dying alone and dirty you had acted with proper decorum. It was time for my bath. I had quite a lengthy bath, got out, walked about the room, glistening, drew up a chair, sat naked beside you and watched you.

   *Pause.*

When I brought him into the room your body of course had gone. What a relief it was to have a different body in my

[ 57 ]

room, a male body behaving quite differently, doing all those things they do and which they think are good, like sitting with one leg over the arm of an armchair. We had a choice of two beds. Your bed or my bed. To lie in, or on. To grind noses together, in or on. He liked your bed, and thought he was different in it because he was a man. But one night I said let me do something, a little thing, a little trick. He lay there in your bed. He looked up at me with great expectation. He was gratified. He thought I had profited from his teaching. He thought I was going to be sexually forthcoming, that I was about to take a long-promised initiative. I dug about in the window box, where you had planted our pretty pansies, scooped, filled the bowl, and plastered his face with dirt. He was bemused, aghast, resisted, resisted with force. He would not let me dirty his face, or smudge it, he wouldn't let me. He suggested a wedding instead and a change of environment

*Slight pause.*

Neither mattered.

*Pause.*

He asked me once, at about that time, who had slept in that bed before him. I told him no one. No one at all.

# Our Country's Good

TIMBERLAKE WERTENBAKER

*First produced at the Royal Court Theatre Downstairs, London, in 1988 with Linda Bassett as Lizzie.*

Timberlake Wertenbaker's play, based on Thomas Keneally's novel *The Playmaker*, which is itself based on fact, is about the transforming power of theatre – not surprising, then, that it is invariably a moving experience for audiences. In 1788/9 a group of convicts – guilty of fairly minor offences – are transported to Sydney, Australia. Once there, the officers, many of whom have slept with the women convicts on the boat, are divided as to how their charges should be treated. Some feel they are no more than animals to be kept locked up; others that they should be taught practical skills; and a few that they would benefit from taking part in a play. Despite the sniggering and hostility, it falls to Second Lieutenant Ralph Clark to stage Farquhar's *The Recruiting Officer*. As he rehearses, a group of disparate convicts slowly become engrossed in the process of becoming someone else and speaking another person's words. Lizzie is an aggressive, illiterate Londoner who is described as being 'lower than a slave, full of loathing, foul-mouthed, desperate'. She frightens the other convicts and is widely assumed to be destined for the gallows, but even so she is cast in the significant role of Melinda, an assured, rich young lady. Rehearsals are muddling along when a group of officers arrive with the news that some of the men have tried to run away and that Lizzie was seen helping them to steal some food from the stores. The evidence is weak, but Lizzie at first won't defend herself, whether out of fatalism, pride, or some kind of honour among thieves. In this scene, Lizzie faces the prospect of being hanged and describes her education in crime. She speaks in a kind of thieves' cant but her meaning is clear, particularly her betrayal by her father. It is as if she herself feels that her life is worthless. In the end, she does defend herself and startlingly promises the Governor that she will 'endeavour to speak Mr Farquhar's lines with the elegance and clarity their own worth commands'. Speaking in another person's voice has helped her to find her own. She is released and triumphantly takes part in the play.

*shifts its bob* – gets out of way
*ha'penny planet* – unlucky star
*nibbler* – petty thief
*crapped* – hanged
*titter* – daughter
*shoulder-clapped* – arrested
*prig* – steal
*trine for a make . . . wap for a winne* – why hang for a ha'penny when you can whore for a penny?
*dimber mort, swell mollisher* – beauty, good-looking woman
*mother of saints* – cunt
*swell cove* – gentleman
*bobcull* – good-natured fellow
*mossie face* – cunt
*shiners* – newly minted coins
*spice the swells* – rob the rich
*lifts* – steals
*stir my stumps* – run away
*squeaks beef* – gives the alarm
*snoozie* – a night constable
*nibbed* – arrested
*up the ladder to rest* – off to be hanged
*fortune-teller* – judge
*nap the King's pardon* – get reprieved from hanging
*seven years across the herring pond* – Liz was sentenced to seven years' transportation
*rantum scantum* – sex
*nob it* – prosper
*rufflers* – rogues

**Liz** Luck? Don't know the word. Shifts its bob when I comes near. Born under a ha'penny planet I was. Dad's a nibbler, don't want to get crapped. Mum leaves. Five brothers, I'm the only titter. I takes in washing. Then. My own father. Lady's walking down the street, he takes her wiper. She screams, says he's shoulder-clapped, it's not me, Sir, it's Lizzie, look, she took it. I'm stripped, beaten in the street, everyone watching. That night, I take my dad's cudgel and try to kill him. I prig all his clothes and go to my older brother. He don't want me. Liz, he says, why trine for a make, when you can wap for a winne? I'm no dimber mort, I says. Don't ask you to be a swell mollisher, Sister, men want Miss Laycock, don't look at your mug. So I begin to sell my mother of saints. I thinks I'm in luck when I meet the swell cove. He's a bobcull: sports a different wiper every day of the week. He says to me, it's not enough to sell your mossie face, Lizzie, it don't bring no shiners no more. Shows me how to spice the swells. So Swell has me up the wall, flashes a pocket watch, I lifts it. But one time, I stir my stumps too slow, the swell squeaks beef, the snoozie hears. I'm nibbed. It's up the ladder to rest, I thinks, when I goes up before the fortune-teller, but no, the judge's a bobcull, I nap the King's pardon and it's seven years across the herring pond. Jesus Christ the hunger on the ship, sailors won't touch me: no rantum scantum, no food. But here, the Governor says, new life. You could nob it here, Lizzie, I thinks, bobcull Gov, this niffynaffy play, not too much work, good crew of rufflers, Kable, Arscott, but no, Ross don't like my mug, I'm nibbed again and now it's up the ladder to rest for good.

# Outlying Islands

DAVID GREIG

*First produced at the Traverse Theatre, Edinburgh, in 2002
with Lesley Hart as Ellen.*

David Greig's play is set on the eve of the Second World War.
Two young ornithologists, Robert and John, are sent by the
government to one of the outlying islands off Scotland. Robert
has a brilliant, objective mind; John is more of a plodder and
swayed by others' opinions. They believe that their task is to
record the unique bird life that inhabits the island. In fact the
government wants to know whether the place is suitable for
experimenting with anthrax, for use in warfare, a task that
would destroy rather than preserve the wildlife. The arrange-
ment to stay has been made with Kirk, a God-fearing man
who owns the island and is greedily looking forward to a large
compensation cheque when the government moves in. Kirk
lives with his niece, Ellen, who has led a sheltered life and is
hungry to know more about the world and especially about
men. Most of her information comes from trips to the cinema
on the mainland – hence the reference to Laurel and Hardy.
A Darwinian struggle for survival follows between Kirk and
the visitors, who are appalled at the thought of the island
being destroyed, and between John and Robert for Ellen.
Cut off from the mainland, the civilised rules of society no
longer seem to apply. When Kirk dies from a heart attack
largely as a consequence of Robert's physical assault, there
are no authorities to deal with the case. Not even Ellen grieves
that much, but rather relishes her new freedom as is shown
by this very sexy speech. As Robert says of nature: 'Death
means more room for the young.' Here, she describes seeing
Robert preening himself in the sun before diving naked into
the sea.

**Ellen**  I sat with the body for three days and three nights and on the morning of the third day I rose from a half-dream and came out from the ground and into the daylight. I walked to the good well looking for water to wash and I saw the boy –

I see him at the cliff top standin' like he's got a thought in his head a thought like a midge botherin' him and he's looking away away out over the blackness of the sea towards the mainland where we've come from and I'm thinking why's he come here this boy this boy to stand on this cliff and why's he come all the way here from London from there where all waits for him why's he come and as I'm thinking he vanishes over the cliff edge like he's jumped and I so I howk up my skirts and go over to see where he's gone and I find the cliffs not sheer as it looks but sheep-pathed and he's running or more like falling down through the gannetry with the birds raising hell about him and stabbing for his head and the fulmars spitting oil at him and the noise and eggs falling and he's waving his hands about him and laughing and shrieking like he's found his own family and at last he reaches the water's edge where the sea swell's rising and falling and sucking and blowing at the rocks and I'm thinking he'll have trouble climbing back up here and I'm half away to fetch my uncle with his long rope for the fowling when I remember that uncle's dead and cold in the pagan chapel lying way way out of reach of me and so I stand and I remain watching and the boy starts to stripping his shirt and trousers from him his body white and skinny and he strips it all, he strips off all his clothes and they lie in the puddle of hot sun about him and I watch him and he doesn't know and he closes his eyes and his hands fall to touching himself to the giving of himself pleasure and there in the hot sun on the rock like a young gull preening I watch him and I'm thinking this is the thing of the most beauty I have ever seen this badness this fallen thought and I want to drink it this moment like a draught of whisky when the boy rises from the rock and all of a sudden dives into the sea and the boy swims the twenty yards it takes him to the stack of rock where he comes out and shakes himself down and he shivers the water from him and I think I think I think what is this feeling I'm having here this feeling of affection that's rising in me what is this feeling and I'm thinking this when all of a sudden he touches his hair and pulls it from his black gull eyes and he looks right at me and I realise –

This affection is an affection I have felt before.

This affection has come to me in my dreams before.

This is the same feeling, the way two sorrows can be the same the same affection as I have felt thirty-seven times in the darkness.

It is the affection I have felt for Stan Laurel.

Beautiful and tender, Stan Laurel.

And that is what I saw.

# The People are Friendly

MICHAEL WYNNE

*First produced at the Royal Court Theatre Downstairs, London, in 2002 with Michelle Butterly as Donna.*

Michael Wynne's *The People are Friendly* revolves around two sisters and their different perceptions of Liverpool. Michelle, her father's favourite, was the one who got away and has had a well-paid successful career in London: Donna, a mother at sixteen, never left. Now in her early thirties, she works in a peanut factory and is struggling to keep her family together: a drunken partner; a drug-dealing, celebrity-obsessed daughter who is also a teenage mother; and a son, Eddie, who refuses to speak. Unbeknown to Donna, Eddie has been killing all the pets in the neighbourhood. Worried by this massacre, Donna imagines that there are evil spirits everywhere. 'All men have ever done,' says Donna, 'is fuck things up.' It's difficult to know how her family would cope without her tremendous efforts.

Tired of London, Michelle applies for a job in order to come back to Liverpool – one that involves redeveloping the area where the ships used to be built and where her father used to work. He has been depressed ever since he was made redundant. Michelle and her boyfriend are able to buy a vast house close to the estate where Donna and her parents still live. Michelle believes that she is returning to a city where old-fashioned values have not died, where the people are friendly and have time to stop for a chat: in fact, the whole community is falling apart. Even in Michelle's posh street one of her neighbours is selling drugs to her niece. The play takes place on one disastrous day in which Michelle invites her whole family over to see the house and have lunch. She gives them fancy food to eat, including stuffed vine-leaves that Donna refers to as 'six shits on a plate'. There is considerable tension between Michelle and Donna; all Michelle's efforts to impress are met with scorn. Finally, Michelle lets slip the details of her new job. She believes that the redevelopment of Liverpool will improve everyone's lives, not just those who can afford the fancy sea-view apartments. Near the end of the play, Donna sets her straight. All her fury – frustration as well as resentment – pours out. A convincing Liverpudlian accent is essential!

**Donna** What do you know about reality? What sort of
reality do you live in? Eh? Where all you've got to worry
about is the street being too crowded and you're late for a
meeting. Or the Tube being a bit smelly. This is reality. My
family is reality. A psycho child who's got me wrapped
round his little finger. A lazy depressed fella and a daughter
who thinks she's Britney fuckin' Spears. My reality is
working nights and split shifts packing fuckin' peanuts.
Paying one loan off with another, buying everything off the
catalogue in fifty-two weekly instalments. The reality of
having to borrow two quid off your mum till the end of the
week. Trying to keep it all together. And it's all down to me,
no one else. If I stop for one minute, it all falls apart . . .

A lot's changed since you lived 'ere, it's getting worse and
we don't need people like you coming back 'ere telling us
how to live . . .

But you know what we've got, we've got the best thing
anyone could want. We've got friendly people . . .

Why would we need good jobs or a future because the
bloke on the bus says thank you when you get off and
people hold the door open for y' in Asda? Life just can't get
any better for me . . .

Why did you come back, eh? To rub our faces in it? To
fuck us up the arse?

# Portia Coughlan

## MARINA CARR

*First produced at the Abbey Theatre, Dublin, and the Royal Court Theatre, London, in 1996 with Derbhle Crotty as Portia.*

London theatre in the nineties was notable for the massive contribution made by Irish playwrights – Martin McDonagh, Conor McPherson, and Marina Carr most especially. Carr's *Portia Coughlan* is dominated by a wild thirty-year-old who is careering towards disaster. Portia, like her Shakespearean namesake, lives in a place called Belmont, but that's about all they have in common. She and her brother Gabriel were uncomfortably close even for twins. Fifteen years ago, Gabriel drowned himself in the Belmont River, watched by his sister. We are never quite sure whether Portia intended to follow him and changed her mind. On her thirtieth birthday, she is wearing a nightshirt at ten o'clock in the morning and is surrounded by dirty dishes. She is drunk, desperate, depressed, and haunted by Gabriel, who is more real for her dead than anyone alive. Her despised husband, mother, father and lover feel the lash of her tongue. She refuses to have anything to do with her children because, she later reveals, she's afraid that she may harm them. She wants to leave home, but every day she is drawn back to the river, to the spot where Gabriel died. Her patient, uninspiring and wealthy husband tries to persuade her to seek help. It is no surprise when Portia throws herself in the river. Although not without a certain raucous humour, there are times when Carr's play feels as if it should be set in ancient Greece rather than Ireland; at others it feels like some terrible family tragedy described in the newspapers. The play is oddly structured: the winching of Portia's body out of the water and her funeral take place in between the events of her birthday. In this speech near the beginning of the play, Portia is at home and recalling in her thick Irish Midlands accent, her previous night's dream to her mother.

**Portia**  He would've been thirty today as well – sometimes
I think only half of me is left, the worst half. Do ya know
the only reason I married Raphael? Not because you and
Daddy says I should, not because he was rich, I care nothin'
for money, naw. The only reason I married Raphael was
because of his name, a angel's name, same as Gabriel's, and
I thought be osmosis or just pure wishin' that one'd take
on the qualities of the other. But Raphael is not Gabriel and
never will be – And I dreamt about him again last night,
was one of them dreams as is so real you think it's actually
happenin'. Gabriel had come to dinner here and after he
got up to leave and I says, 'Gabriel, stay for the weekend,'
but Gabriel demurs out of politeness to me and Raphael.
And I says, 'Gabriel, it's me, Portia, your twin, don't be
polite, there's no need with me' – And then he turns and
smiles and I know he's goin' to stay and me heart blows
open and stars falls out of me chest as happens in dreams –
We were so alike, weren't we, Mother? . . .
     Came out of the womb holdin' hands – When God was
handin' out souls he must've got mine and Gabriel's mixed
up, aither that or he gave us just the one between us and it
went into the Belmont River with him – Oh, Gabriel, ya had
no right to discard me so, to float me on the world as if
I were a ball of flotsam. Ya had no right.

*Begins to weep uncontrollably.*

# The Positive Hour

## APRIL DE ANGELIS

*First produced by Out of Joint Theatre Company at
Hampstead Theatre, London, in 1997 with Julia Lane as
Paula.*

Paula is just one of the reasons why Miranda, the leading
character in April De Angelis's play, is having a breakdown.
Miranda is a social worker, a feminist and liberal humanist.
Both in her personal life and in her work she finds that emo-
tional forces are taking over. Paula, one of her clients, is des-
perate to be reunited with her daughter, who has been placed
with foster-parents. In order to get Victoria back, she has to
move out of temporary accommodation, give up prostitution,
and show her abusive boyfriend the door. It's a tall order,
and if she is to succeed she needs instant rewards. Paula is
far from being stupid but she's at the mercy of her violent
temper and finds it hard to consider her plight as rationally
as her social worker would wish. Paula is tempted to mock
when she unwillingly attends one of Miranda's women's
groups. She doesn't accept that together the women in the
group can be stronger than any one of them individually, nor
does she believe that she can rise above the malignant forces
that invariably bring her down. Miranda is finally defeated
by the irrationality that surrounds her at the end of the play.
Paula and Nicole, another of Miranda's clients, do, however,
begin to give each other support. Near the beginning of the
play, Paula reports back to Miranda that she has taken her
social worker's advice and thrown her boyfriend out. In return
she needs results rather than Miranda's cautious response. A
few lines later she says: 'I have to have something, Miranda.
I can't stay in that room with less than I had before.'

**Paula** Well, I did it. This is how I did it. I drank neat vodka. Then I taped a note to my door which said, 'It's over, love Paula.' Then I left his reproduction Armani underpants in a plastic bag on the mat. Then I hid. Mastermind. Only I never closed my window. Two a.m., I wake up and he's looming over me. 'Fuck you, Paula,' he said. 'Fuck you, Michael,' I said. That went on for a bit. I said, 'I'm sorry, Michael, but what can I do? I have to demonstrate my desire to provide a good home for my daughter.' He tried snogging. It didn't work. Well, it did for about two minutes. But, anyway. Cut to me an hour later. More vodka had been swilled. More tears had watered the ashtray. I was doing it. I didn't even know why I was doing it. Finally, I took the taped note off the door and stuck it on my forehead. I said, 'Michael, it's not that I don't think you're a decent bloke underneath, but who's got a spade big enough to shovel off all the shit?'

*She turns slightly to one side.*

That's how I got my eye. This morning I woke up and I swear I felt like Bambi. I lay there for a bit just listening to the sounds coming in the window and I thought, this is nice.

# Proof

## DAVID AUBURN

*First produced at the Manhattan Theatre Club, New York City, in 2000 with Mary-Louise Parker as Catherine.*

*Proof* takes maths as its subject although, thankfully for most theatregoers, no maths are required to follow the play. It was a huge hit in New York, transferring from the Manhattan Theatre Club to Broadway in 2000. In London, it played at the Donmar Warehouse with Gwyneth Paltrow as Catherine. The 'proof' of the title contrasts the precision of a mathematical equation with the messiness of life and the need, sometimes, to make a great leap of faith. Catherine, a twenty-five-year-old living in Chicago, has inherited her father's exceptional talent for maths. Her fear is that she may have inherited his instability as well – a fear exacerbated in the first scene by a visit from her father's ghost on the eve of his funeral.

The play switches between the events following the funeral and Catherine's life with her father. Once admired as an exceptional mathematician by all his university colleagues, he spends his last years compulsively filling notebooks with nothing but rubbish. Catherine gives up her own place at university to look after him. One of the most poignant moments of the play occurs when he passes Catherine one of these books in the belief that he has made a recovery. She seizes it eagerly, but all hope drains out of her face as she reads the nonsense he has written.

After Robert's death, Hal, who was once one of Robert's geeky students, is determined to go through the notebooks and see if there is anything worth salvaging. His hero-worshipping of Robert offends Catherine, who has had to deal with the real man and not the legend, and his reaction provokes the speech below. Later the two go to bed together and she shows him some of her own work. Neither he nor her sister, who visits from New York for the funeral, can believe that Catherine is capable of such original research and Hal's lack of trust drives her into depression.

**Catherine** *I lived with him.*

I spent my life with him. I fed him. Talked to him. Tried to listen when he talked. Talked to people who weren't there . . . Watched him shuffling around like a ghost. A very smelly ghost. He was filthy. I had to make sure he bathed. My own father . . .

After my mother died it was just me here. I tried to keep him happy no matter what idiotic project he was doing. He used to read all day. He kept demanding more and more books. I took them out of the library by the car load. We had hundreds upstairs. Then I realised he wasn't reading: he believed aliens were sending him messages through the Dewey decimal numbers on the library books. He was trying to work out the code . . .

Beautiful mathematics. The most elegant proofs, perfect proofs, proofs like music . . .

Plus fashion tips, knock-knock jokes – I mean it was *nuts*, OK?

Later the writing phase: scribbling nineteen, twenty hours a day . . . I ordered him a case of notebooks and he used every one.

I dropped out of school . . .

I'm glad he's dead.

# RolePlay

from *Damsels in Distress*

## ALAN AYCKBOURN

*First produced at the Stephen Joseph Theatre, Scarborough, in 2001, transferring to the Duchess Theatre, London, with Alison Pargeter as Paige.*

*RolePlay* is part of a trilogy by Alan Ayckbourn called *Damsels in Distress*, in which each of the plays is set in the same Docklands flat although with different characters. Paige makes one of the most spectacular entrances in British drama. She is first heard screaming and then seen hanging on for grim life from the balcony of a Docklands flat, inch by inch painfully pulling her head above the parapet in the driving rain. She is in her late twenties, soaked to the skin, covered in blood, and on the run from Micky, her minder, who is in a flat above. Rudy Raven, a boxing promoter and her violent lover, has given strict orders that she should be kept locked up. Her abrupt arrival is a disruptive influence on a momentous occasion in the lives of Justin and Julie-Ann, who have invited her parents and his alcoholic mother to dinner in order to announce their engagement. The potential in-laws are meeting for the first time. Paige divides the guests in that Julie-Ann's ghastly parents – he is a boorish, racist bully with a bad line in jokes to which she titters obligingly – are appalled by Paige's juicy revelations about her past, while Justin's mother admires her spirit and drunkenly insists on treating her, rather than Julie-Ann, as her future daughter-in-law. Paige is an unpredictable life force compared to Julie-Ann's dreary conformity, and Justin increasingly begins to have doubts about his choice of wife. Paige is attracted to Justin too, and in desperation she pretends here that she comes from a smart family and that her London accent has been acquired much later in life. Nobody is convinced.

**Paige** (*suddenly*) I didn't always talk like this. I used to talk very, very posh indeed because I come originally from this amazingly smart family. They were real upper-class. Only when I was sixteen, see, I was riding on the back of my boyfriend's motorbike only we weren't wearing helmets and we hit this hole in the road doing about seventy-five and we were both hurled sixty feet into a brick wall and he was killed outright and I was in a coma for eighteen months . . .

And when I finally came to, my memory was completely gone. My head was totally empty. I didn't know who I was or anything. They told me I was like a child of two. And I had to be taught everything, all over again. How to talk, how to write, how to feed myself. I even had to learn how to go to the toilet. And I had this one nurse that taught me everything, you see. Everything. Only she talked like this. So subsequently when I learnt to talk again, I talked like her. Like this. Only if she'd been Welsh or Scottish, I'd probably have had a Taffy accent, you see. Or Scotch.

*Silence.*

I never told anyone that before.

# The Secret Rapture

DAVID HARE

*First produced at the National Theatre, London, in 1988 with Clare Higgins as Katherine.*

David Hare's play opens with a bedroom scene in which Isobel is sitting in the dark by her father's corpse. She is seeking time and space in which to grieve when she is interrupted by her older sister Marion, come to retrieve a ring she had given her father in a fit of generosity. They are very different people: Marion is a go-getting, combative junior minister in Mrs Thatcher's government; Isobel is more tolerant, a generous woman who endeavours to see the best in everyone. Their father, an unworldly owner of a bookshop and member of CND, has left an alcoholic widow in her late twenties. Marion regards her as a problem to be removed. Isobel remembers that her father felt that the only thing that distinguished his life was his late passion for this younger woman. Katherine is self-destructive, wilful, and her behaviour often outrageous. She depends on others to rescue her from a succession of disasters. She latches on to Isobel, demanding a job in her graphic design company. Having lived on the wild side, Katherine thinks she is a tough woman of the world, unlike the more idealistic Isobel, but in fact her interference in the company is disastrous, the final straw being an attempt to stab a would-be client in the heart. She fortunately misses. As Isobel uncharacteristically comments: 'He's an ad-man. He's got a very small heart.'

The passage below takes place early on in the play on the day of the funeral at which they are all pretending to enjoy drinking squash to help Katherine keep off the bottle. She has just announced her intention of working with Isobel, much to the latter's surprise. Katherine reacts badly when

Isobel suggests that she will have to consult her colleagues before anything can be decided, and that they may not be able to afford another employee. Katherine storms out, returning later in a more placatory mood having discovered where Marion's husband has hidden the bottle.

**Katherine** I've spoken to Mrs Hurley. I was in the kitchen. Lunch will be ready in three-quarters of an hour. She's planning a rabbit-and-vegetable pie . . .

I outsmarted him. I've hidden the bottle again . . .

It gives me confidence, and I must say today I should be allowed a little confidence. Given what lies ahead.

*She smiles bravely, wiping her eyes with her sleeve. She sits down.*

Your dad never told you, he actually met me when he stopped one night in a motel. It was in the Vale of Evesham, he was coming back from the North. I don't know how I'd ended up there. I was working the bar. It was appalling. Trying to pick men up – not even for money, but because I was so unhappy with myself. I wanted something to happen. I don't know how I thought these men might help me, they were travellers, small goods, that sort of thing, all with slack bellies and smelling of late-night curries. I can still smell them. I don't know why, I'd been doing it for weeks. Then Robert came in. He said, 'I'll drive you to Gloucestershire. It will give you some peace.' He brought me here, to this house. He put fresh sheets in the spare room. Everything I did, before or since, he forgave.

*She sits, tears in her eyes, quiet now.*

People say I took advantage of his decency. But what are good people for? They're here to help the trashy people like me.

# Skylight

## DAVID HARE

*First produced at the National Theatre, London, in 1995
with Lia Williams as Kyra.*

David Hare's play is a highly charged romance, but also political in that so much of the eighties comes under the microscope. Kyra is just past thirty. Hare describes her as being 'quite small, with short hair and a practical manner'. She lives in a grotty flat in Kilburn in London and travels laboriously by bus every day across the city to East Ham to teach in an under-achieving school. In the past she enjoyed a more luxurious lifestyle when she worked in Tom's thriving restaurants and was taken in to live with his family. Tom and Kyra began an affair, but when Tom's wife discovered that her husband was being unfaithful, Kyra disappeared. Since then the wife has died. Tom and Kyra have not seen each other for three years when he turns up unexpectedly on a snowy night at her flat. Their exchanges are initially barbed. Fifty-year-old Tom is used to the good things in life and can't understand why Kyra has chosen to live in such scruffy surroundings. He talks of his business, of the death of his wife, his relationship with his son, and finally of the depth of his feeling for Kyra. Throughout this exchange, his chauffeur is waiting outside. Horrified to discover this, Kyra insists that he is sent away and, inevitably, she and Tom go to bed together.

The second act takes place in the middle of the night when Kyra gets up to do some marking. Tom joins her. He is now pleased with his conquest and rather more rash in his comments. He attacks Kyra for her chosen career. He feels that she is deliberately choosing a martyr-like role for herself, preferring to live on one side of London and work on another, choosing to freeze rather than buy a proper heater. He accuses her of female stubbornness. Finally, in the following speech, she is goaded into a response, making it clear that she sees her life as a reaction to the Thatcherite values which Tom embraces.

**Kyra** 'Female'? That's a very odd choice of word.

*He knows that he has betrayed a source of his anger and she at once has an ascendancy in the argument with him. She picks the books up off the floor and begins regretfully.*

You see I'm afraid I think this is typical. It's something that's happened . . . it's only happened of late. That people should need to ask why I'm helping these children. I'm helping them because they need to be helped.

*Tom turns away unconvinced by the simplicity of the answer, but she is already moving back to the table with the books, her anger beginning to rise.*

Everyone makes merry, discussing motive. Of course she does this. She works in the East End. She only does it because she's unhappy. She does it because of a lack in herself. She doesn't have a man. If she had a man, she wouldn't need to do it. Do you think she's a dyke? She must be fucked up, she must be an Amazon, she must be a weirdo to choose to work where she does . . . Well, I say, what the hell does it matter why I'm doing it? Why anyone goes out and helps? The reason is hardly of primary importance. If I didn't do it, it wouldn't get done.

*She is now suddenly so passionate, so forceful that Tom is silenced.*

I'm tired of these sophistries. I'm tired of these right-wing fuckers. They wouldn't lift a finger themselves. They work contentedly in offices and banks. Yet now they sit pontific-ating in parliament, in papers, impugning our motives, questioning our judgements. And why? Because they themselves need to feel better by putting down everyone whose work is so much harder than theirs.

*She stands, nodding.*

You only have to. say the words 'social worker' . . . 'probation officer' . . . 'counsellor' . . . for everyone in this country to sneer. Do you know what social workers do? Every day? They try and clear out society's drains. They clear out the rubbish. They do what no one else is doing, what no one else is willing to do. And for that, oh Christ, do we thank them? No, we take our own rotten consciences, wipe them all over the social worker's face, and say, 'If . . .' FUCK! 'If *I* did the job, then of course if I did it . . . oh no, excuse me, I wouldn't do it like that . . .'

*She turns, suddenly aggressive.*

Well, I say: 'OK, then, fucking do it, journalist. Politician, talk to the addicts. Hold families together. Stop the kids from stealing in the streets. Deal with couples who beat each other up. You fucking try it, why not? Since you're so full of advice. Sure, come and join us. This work is one big casino. By all means. Anyone can play. But there's only one rule. You can't play for nothing. You have to buy some chips to sit at the table. And if you won't pay with your own time . . . with your own effort . . . then I'm sorry. Fuck off!'

# Three Birds Alighting on a Field

TIMBERLAKE WERTENBAKER

*First produced at the Royal Court Theatre Downstairs,
London, in 1991 with Harriet Walter as Biddy.*

Timberlake Wertenbaker's satire on the art world was a breath
of fresh air in 1991, a clever and witty criticism of Thatcher-
ism and market values. Biddy's monologue is only the second
scene of the play – the first sees a 'totally flat, authentically
white' canvas being sold by an auctioneer for over £1 million.
Biddy introduces herself to the audience as an upper-class,
middle-aged, conventional woman, very familiar with Chel-
sea – the area around the Royal Court – and used to being
either patronised or ignored. But after her second marriage
to Yoyo, a Greek millionaire property developer, she finds
that her new wealth changes the way people feel about her.
Suddenly everyone hangs on her every word, treating her
most banal comments as hugely significant. Ordered by her
husband to acquire 'an interior life' in order to smooth his
passage into English society, Biddy becomes genuinely inter-
ested in contemporary art. While Wertenbaker shows how
the galleries are hugely influenced by fashion, marketing and
the performance of the stock markets, Biddy grows in confi-
dence as she learns to trust her own eyes and falls for the
English landscapes of Stephen Ryle (think William Tillyer).
In the first production, Harriet Walter played Biddy. For the
Royal Court audience, this character was a novelty. The upper
classes are often caricatured in Royal Court plays. Here, audi-
ences began by laughing at Biddy and then were surprised to
find themselves laughing with her.

**Biddy** I didn't at first understand what was happening.
For someone like me, who was used to being tolerated, it
came as a surprise. You see, before, everything I said was
passed over. Well, smiled at, but the conversation would
continue elsewhere. I was like the final touches of a well-
decorated house. It gives pleasure, but you don't notice it.
The sound of my voice was what mattered, it made people
feel secure: England still had women who went to good
schools, and looked after large homes in the country, horses,
dogs, children, that sort of thing, that was my voice. Tony –
that's my first husband – said he found my conversation
comforting background noise when he read the papers.

But then, silences began to greet everything I said. Heavy
silences. I thought there was something wrong. Then I noticed
they were waiting for more words, and these words had
suddenly taken on a tremendous importance. But I was still
saying the same things. You know, about shopping at
Harrod's, and trains being slow, and good avocados being
hard to come by, and cleaning ladies even harder. And then,
I understood.

You see, I had become tremendously rich. Not myself,
but my husband, my second husband. And when you're
that rich, nothing you do is trivial. If I took an hour telling
a group of people how I had looked for and not found a
good pair of gardening gloves, if I went into every detail of
the weeks I had spent on this search, the phone bills I had
run up, the catalogues I had returned, they were absolutely
riveted. Riveted.

Because it seemed everything I did, now that I was so
tremendously rich because of my second husband, mattered.
Mattered tremendously. I hadn't expected this, because you

see, my husband was foreign, Greek actually, and I found that not – well, not quite properly English, you know, to be married to a Greek – after all, Biddy *Andreas*? I could imagine my headmistress – we had a Greek girl at Benenden, we all turned down invitations to her island – and Yoyo – that's my husband, George, Giorgos, actually – he didn't even go to school here – but he was so rich and I became used to it – him and me: being important.

# Wit

MARGARET EDSON

*First produced at the South Coast Repertory Theater,
California, in 1995 with Megan Cole as Vivian Bearing*

Margaret Edson's affecting, Pulitzer-prize-winning play is
about an unmarried, highly respected but feared American
academic memorably played by Kathleen Chalfant in New
York and London. Vivian Bearing, PhD, is a specialist in the
seventeenth-century metaphysical poetry of John Donne, and
her formidable intellect and judgement are unclouded by
sentiment or kindness. At the age of fifty, she discovers she
has a tumour the size of a grapefruit. The diagnosis is stage-
four metastatic ovarian cancer and she embarks on an aggres-
sive programme of chemotherapy. Her rigorous attitude to
her own studies resembles that of the consultants on her case.
Her lack of interest in her students' welfare is matched by
the doctors' inability to take on board the fears of their
patients. What they do notice is that Vivian is more capable
than most of coping with pain, and so is useful for their
experiments. They are ruthless in their desire to test their
theories and try out new treatments.

Apart from the occasional flashback, the play takes place
in the hospital, a new world for Vivian, where words are
casually used instead of being treated with the respect that
she has always given them. Although she tries to be stoical
and as clear-sighted about her treatment as she was once
about her work, she becomes increasingly scared and lonely
– she only has one visitor – and begins to value other quali-
ties apart from a fine mind, especially the kindness of her
nurse who strokes her hand and speaks to her like a human
being rather than an interesting specimen.

There can be no doubt in the audience's mind that Vivian is going to die – indeed she announces her death in the speech which follows, taken from the beginning of the play when she appears in a red baseball cap to cover her bald head and pushing an IV drip-pole. It's not surprising that most performances are accompanied by the sound of sniffles and sobs in the audience.

**Vivian** (*in false familiarity, waving and nodding to the audience*) Hi. How are you feeling today? Great. That's just great.

*In her own professorial tone.*

This is not my standard greeting, I assure you.

I tend toward something a little more formal, a little less inquisitive, such as, say, 'Hello.'

But it is the standard greeting here.

There is some debate as to the correct response to this salutation. Should one reply, 'I feel good,' using 'feel' as a copulative to link the subject, 'I,' to its subjective complement, 'good'; or, 'I feel well,' modifying with an adverb the subject's state of being?

I don't know. I am a professor of seventeenth-century poetry, specialising in the Holy Sonnets of John Donne.

So I just say, 'Fine.'

Of course it is not very often that I do feel fine.

I have been asked, 'How are you feeling today?' while I was throwing up into a plastic washbasin. I have been asked as I was emerging from a four-hour operation with a tube in every orifice, 'How are you feeling today?'

I am waiting for the moment when someone asks me this question and I am dead.

I'm a little sorry I'll miss that.

It is unfortunate that this remarkable line of inquiry has come to me so late in my career. I could have exploited its feigned solicitude to great advantage: as I was distributing the final examination to the graduate course in seventeenth-century textual criticism – 'Hi. How are you feeling today?'

Of course I would not be wearing this costume at the time, so the question's *ironic significance* would not be fully apparent.

As I trust it is now.

*Irony* is a literary device that will necessarily be deployed to great effect.

I ardently wish this were not so. I would prefer that a play about me be cast in the mythic-heroic-pastoral mode; but the facts, most notably stage-four metastatic ovarian cancer, conspire against that. *The Faerie Queen* this is not.

And I was dismayed to discover that the play would contain elements of . . . *humour*.

I have been, at best, an *unwitting* accomplice.

*She pauses.*

It is not my intention to give away the plot; but I think I die at the end.

They've given me less than two hours.

If I were poetically inclined, I might employ a threadbare metaphor – the sands of time slipping through the hourglass, the two-hour glass.

Now our sands are almost run;
More a little, and then dumb.

Shakespeare. I trust the name is familiar.

At the moment, however, I am disinclined to poetry.

I've got less than two hours. Then: curtain.

# Yard Gal

REBECCA PRICHARD

*First produced by Clean Break Theatre Company at
the Royal Court Theatre Upstairs (then based at the
Ambassadors), London, in 1998 with Sharon Duncan-
Brewster as Boo.*

Rebecca Prichard's *Yard Gal* was written under the demanding
conditions prescribed by Clean Break, the company founded
by ex-women prisoners. Prichard spent nine months visiting
and running writing workshops at Bullwood Hall prison and
then fulfilled her brief to write a play with an all-female cast
on the topic of female offenders that was suitable to tour
prisons as well as more conventional venues. The two girls in
*Yard Gal* are best friends: Marie, who is white with a violent
father, and the more needy Boo, who is black and con-
demned to living in a hated children's home. They both speak
in a London-Caribbean argot and, talking directly to the
audience, graphically bring to life the other four members of
their posse. There are many plays written about male gangs,
girl gangs are more unusual. Marie and Boo live on the wild
side in their beloved Hackney, spending their days 'tiefin',
getting legless and laid, smoking ganja and starting fights. At
Trenz, the nightclub where people only go 'to get out of their
box, have a dance and have a shag', Marie is egged on to
attack the leader of another gang with a broken bottle. She
escapes but somebody grasses on Boo, who is blamed for the
attack and given two years. Under the pressure of prison and
Marie's pregnancy, their friendship begins to fall apart.

Given the nature of the play and Prichard's skilful story-
telling, there are any number of speeches made by both Marie
and Boo that would make excellent audition pieces. This one,
near the ending, is quite sombre after the ferocity and energy

that has gone before. Boo is sitting in prison wondering why her best friend hasn't been to see her.

*Boo drags her chair slightly apart from Marie.*

**Boo**  Friends are the people who wanna take care of you
and you wanna take care of them innit. I never thought if
I went down it would be by one of my mates grassing me.
But I know it weren't Marie. It was Threse. She hate me
since that fight. The only way she see a friend is someone
who agrees with her, and hypes her up. Otherwise watch
your back. Sometimes I think about the girls on the outside
and what they doing. Smoking up, doing their crime,
getting fucked, drinking and dossing innit. Probably waking
up going that they're bored. Man they should come in 'ere
then they know what bored is. In here I got mates but it
ain't the same. I smoke enuff weed with everyone and chat
and that but here everyone is wanting to get in ya business.
Just 'cos they bored. And they wanna stir it and make
trouble for you to 'ave power over you. They think they
know and they don't, ya know? Sometimes I play games
with meself in my cell. I got a little window that looks at
the block opposite me. Sometimes I count all the windows
in the opposite block and I divide it by the time I got left
and I think how all of us was doing the same time we'd
be out tomorrow but we ain't, we're all doing our own
time. I got twenty-three months left. I only been here
a month and it's already doing my head in. They said it
was 'wounding, with malicious intent'. I got two years.
Everything went silent in my head. I felt the world was
silent when they told me. But I fronted it out. 'Do ya bird'
is what they say. I'll do it standing on my head. Marie said
she'll stick by me but she's full of shit. She said she'll come
and visit but she don't. I don't even know if she think of me

or if she leave me in here to rot. But I miss Marie, you know. I think about her and I even worry about her sometimes. I think about what if she has a fit and I ain't there. I think about what if she's out by herself. I even want to tell her, "Don't go out by yourself." Who's gonna look after her? On the street people will walk away or mug her. When I get out I'm gonna find her even though she ain't been to visit me. I thought she would. But I still find her when I get out. She's my friend from time. My best friend. Yeah Marie. You're nice. Yesterday I wrote Marie a letter:

'Dear Marie,

'I heard you phone and ask for me number. I'm in fucking prison man you can't be telling the screws to get me, they ain't fuckin' British Telecom. Eight o'clock means in my room banged up. Can ya write to me and tell me what's going on? I jus wanna hear about wha's happenin' outside or visit me. Why ain't you come visit me man?

'In here it's fucking rules everywhere. I change me sheets every day and go for medicine twice a day. I get so many pills man. Everyone else is gone and I'm still sitting by the trolley trying to down them all. In here I get tablets for being a paranoid schizophrenic. You always knew I's a nutter didn't ya?

'The screws in here you can't tell if they're men or women. Some of the screws are alright as it goes. If I'm stressed out they'll come and chat to me, have a laugh, sometimes they'll even give me a proper fag. But some of 'em love their fucking keys. How sad innit.

'When I think about that night at Trenz you was so fucking gone. There was more people there who could have stop you. But they egg you on. I know if I was there I would have stop you.

'I miss you Marie, why ain't you come and visit me?

'Love, Boo.'

# Acknowledgements

All plays are published by Faber and Faber Ltd and/or Faber Inc unless otherwise stated. The editor and publishers gratefully acknowledge permission to reproduce copyright material in this book.

The extracts included in this book may be performed in class and for festivals, auditions and examinations without further permission or payment. However, should you wish to perform any scene in a public performance such as a festival, prizewinners' concert or an entertainment involving the selling of tickets, further permission must be obtained from the correct source. In addition, if you wish to perform a play in part or in its entirety you must seek permission first. No performance may be given unless a licence is first obtained. You will find full details inside the published text and it is essential to adhere to the rules.

As a general rule, the publisher Samuel French Limited controls the amateur performing rights for plays it publishes as well as the amateur rights for many plays professionally controlled by others. Their address is: Samuel French Limited, 52 Fitzroy Street, London WIP 6JR

*Baglady* © Frank McGuinness 1988, 1996; *Been So Long* © Ché Walker, 1998; *The Breath of Life* © David Hare, 2002; *The Country* © Martin Crimp, 2000; *Decadence* © Steven Berkoff, 1981, 1982, 1983, 1986, 1989; *The Fastest Clock in the Universe* © Philip Ridley, 1992, 1997 (originally published by Methuen); *Frozen* © Bryony Lavery, 1998, 2002; *In Flame* © Charlotte Jones, 2000; *The Late Middle Classes* © Simon Gray, 1999 (published by Nick Hern Books, reproduced with kind permission); *Medea Redux* © Neil LaBute, 1999 (originally published in the USA by